Everything Is Possible!

By Nancy Parent
Screenplay by David Magee
Based on the series of books by P. L. Travers

Houghton Mifflin Harcourt
Boston New York

Jack the lamplighter dims the streetlamp
in front of 17 Cherry Tree Lane.

This is the home of
Michael Banks and his
children, John, Annabel,
and little Georgie.

One morning, Michael sends the children to the store. They hurry across the park.

Georgie finds a kite. It gets swept up in the wind.

Mary Poppins appears in the clouds. She floats to the ground on Georgie's kite tail.

The children wonder how she already
knows their names.

Michael and his sister,
Jane, cannot believe who
the children bring home.
It is their childhood
nanny, Mary Poppins.

Mary Poppins stays to
look after the children.
She turns bath time
into an underwater
adventure!

Michael and Jane go to the bank. They look for an important certificate they need to pay a loan.

Meanwhile, Georgie patches his old kite
with one of his father's drawings.

John gets an idea. They
can sell their mother's
china bowl to pay the
loan.

By accident, the bowl falls and breaks. The carriage on the bowl's picture now has a broken wheel.

Mary Poppins, Jack, and the children magically enter the world inside the bowl. They help fix the wheel.

Soon they are all home again. Was it a dream?

The next day, Jack gives everyone a ride
to Topsy's shop. She can fix the bowl.

Then Mary Poppins and the children give
Michael his briefcase at his job.

Later Michael sees the certificate he was looking for! Georgie used it to patch his kite.

Michael must get to the bank to pay the loan before time runs out. Otherwise, the bank will take the family's home.

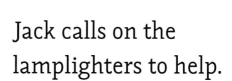

Jack calls on the
lamplighters to help.

The bank doors are locked. Mary Poppins
helps everyone get inside on time.

The bank director says the family can
keep their home.

It is time for Mary Poppins to go. She floats off into the sky!